Mommy, Why Do We Have Easter?

Lou Yohe

Destiny Image® Publishers, Inc.
P.O. Box 310
Shippensburg, PA 17257-0310

"Speaking to the Purposes of God for this Generation
and for the Generations to Come"

ISBN 1-56043-172-5

For Worldwide Distribution
Printed in the U.S.A.

5 6 7 8 9 10 11 12 13 14 / 09 08 07 06 05 04

This book and all other Destiny Image, Revival Press, MercyPlace, Fresh Bread, Destiny Image Fiction, and Treasure House books are available at Christian bookstores and distributors worldwide.

For a U.S. bookstore nearest you, call
1-800-722-6774.

For more information on foreign distributors, call
717-532-3040.

Or reach us on the Internet:
www.destinyimage.com

"Mommy! Mommy!" shouted Jimmy as he ran through the house.

"What's the matter, Jimmy?" asked Mommy.

"Come see what Mrs. Smith is doing to her house!" Jimmy grabbed Mommy's hand and pulled her to the front window. "Isn't that neat? Look at all those decorations. I like that big sign that says 'Happy Easter.' Can we decorate our house for Easter too?"

Mommy was silent for a moment. Then she asked, "Jimmy, why do we celebrate Easter?"

"Oh, Mommy, you know why we celebrate Easter. We talked about it at Sunday school."

Mommy shook her head. "Jimmy, you didn't answer my question. I asked why do we celebrate Easter?"

"To remember that Jesus died for us," Jimmy replied.

"If we celebrate Easter to remember that Jesus died for us, then why should we decorate our house like Mrs. Smith's?" Mommy wanted to know.

"Do I have to answer all these questions?" Jimmy frowned. "Why can't we just decorate our house?"

Jimmy was getting impatient. He pouted a bit as he walked out of the room.

Mommy quietly sat down on the sofa, then called her son to her. "Jimmy, please come here."

Jimmy came, but by the look on his face, she knew that he was still pouting.

"Let's talk about this, Jimmy. I didn't say we couldn't decorate our house. But I think it is important that you understand why we celebrate Easter. Perhaps we need to find out why Easter is a holiday. Let's look in the encyclopedia to see what it says about Easter."

Still not feeling very cooperative, Jimmy said, "Oh, okay."

He sat still and watched as Mommy went to the bookcase and found the volume with an E. Returning to sit beside him, she opened the book. Watching her turn the pages helped Jimmy forget his bad attitude. He started getting excited about what they would find.

"E-A-S-T-E-R," spelled Mommy. "Here it is. Listen while I read to you."

"Easter is a Christian festival that celebrates the resurrection of Jesus Christ. It is the most important holy day of the Christian religion."[1]

Mommy paused. "Jimmy, do you know what resurrection means?" she asked.

"I think...it means that when Jesus died, He came alive again three days later," Jimmy responded. "Wait a minute," he said as he looked up at his mommy with big eyes. "If Easter is for celebrating Jesus' resurrection, then why didn't Mrs. Smith have anything about Jesus around her house? She just had lambs, rabbits, and Easter eggs."

"That's a good question. Let's read some more in the encyclopedia," Mommy answered.

"One legend says that a poor woman dyed some eggs during a famine, and hid them in a nest as an Easter gift for her children. Just as the children discovered the nest, a big rabbit leaped away. The story spread that the rabbit had brought the Easter eggs."[2]

"Mommy, I'll be right back," interrupted Jimmy. He jumped off the sofa and ran out of the living room.

---

[1] *World Book Encyclopedia*, 50th Anniversary Edition, Vol. 6 (Chicago: Field Enterprises Education Corporation, 1966), p. 24.
[2] *World Book Encyclopedia*, Vol. 6, p. 26.

In a flash he returned with his Bible storybook. Quickly he flipped through the pages to the picture of Jesus hanging on the cross.

He stopped and gazed at the picture. He didn't say anything. Mommy sat and watched him for a few minutes. Finally she said, "What are you thinking, Jimmy?"

Jimmy didn't reply immediately, but Mommy waited patiently. Then he said, "Mommy, I want to let everyone know why we celebrate Easter. What Jesus did for us makes Easter the best day of the year. Boy, do people have the wrong reason for celebrating Easter."

"What do you mean?" questioned Mommy.

"Well, Jesus had to die because of the bad things I do. My Sunday school teacher calls it sin," said Jimmy thoughtfully as he turned back the pages to the beginning of the Bible storybook.

He pointed to the picture of Adam and Eve in the Garden of Eden. "First Adam and Eve were happy—then they disobeyed God. That's when sin came." He turned to the next page, which showed the ark with lots of animals around it. "God told Noah to build an ark and the big flood came. But that didn't help because people just wouldn't listen to God. So God had to send Jesus."

Continuing to page through his Bible storybook, he stopped at the picture of Baby Jesus in a manger. "Christmas is Jesus' birthday," Jimmy said.

Jimmy grinned up at his mommy. "Gee, Mommy, I can't believe how much fun I'm having doing all this...what does Daddy call it when he needs to know something?"

"Research," replied Mommy.

"We're doing research just like Daddy," laughed Jimmy.

"I'm amazed at how much you have learned about Jesus," said Mommy, as she gave Jimmy a big hug. "Shall we do some more 'research'?"

Mommy picked up her Bible and said, "Jesus was 33 years old when He was baptized and began His ministry. 'Behold, the Lamb of God who takes away the sin of the world!'[3] John the Baptist spoke these words when he baptized Jesus."

"Is that why a lamb is important to Easter? Mrs. Smith put one on her lawn," said Jimmy.

Mommy nodded and continued. "Jesus went from place to place telling everyone that He was the Son of God. Then one day Jesus told His disciples that He would soon die. While in Jerusalem, the soldiers came and they hung Jesus on the cross. His friends were very sad when He died. But His friends took His body and put it in a tomb."

[3]John 1:29 NAS.

"I remember," said Jimmy. "And the next day was like our Sunday."

"That's right," Mommy agreed. She opened her Bible again and began to read, "'Now on the first day of the week Mary Magdalene came early to the tomb, while it was still dark, and saw the stone already taken away from the tomb.'[4] When Mary went into the tomb, she saw an angel in a white robe. He said, 'You are looking for Jesus who has been crucified. He is not here, for He has risen.'"[5]

[4]John 20:1.
[5]See Matthew 28:1-6.

"Wow! That must have been exciting!" Jimmy exclaimed. "And that happened on the first day of the week. Sunday is our first day of the week, so I guess that's why every Sunday we celebrate that Jesus is in Heaven, getting ready for us to join Him."

"Jimmy," Mommy continued, "I have a suggestion. Since Easter is the most important day for Christians, even more important than Christmas, let's have a Resurrection Party on Easter Sunday. You know how Daddy likes to have a party on 'Super Bowl Sunday,' especially if he thinks his team is going to win. We could celebrate the victory over sin Jesus won for us when He died on the cross and rose again from the dead. What do you think?"

"That's a neat idea," Jimmy shouted as he jumped up and down in excitement.

"So you don't want to decorate the house for Easter?" asked Mommy.

After thinking for a minute, Jimmy looked up at his mommy and said, "Maybe we could make a cross and put it in our yard with a lamb beside it. Daddy could make a sign that says: JESUS WINS! But the party is the best idea. In fact, let's invite Mrs. Smith so she can learn the real reason we celebrate Easter!" Jimmy declared.

Mommy nodded and smiled as Jimmy kept thinking of plans for their Resurrection Party. This year Easter would be a very special day.

The Mommy Why? Series

MOMMY, WHY DO WE HAVE EASTER?
by Lou Yohe.
ISBN 1-56043-172-5

MOMMY, WHY DID JESUS HAVE TO DIE?
by Dian Layton.
ISBN 1-56043-146-6

MOMMY, WHY CAN'T I WATCH THAT TV SHOW?
by Dian Layton.
ISBN 1-56043-148-2

MOMMY, IS GOD AS STRONG AS DADDY?
by Barbara Knoll.
ISBN 1-56043-150-4

**MOMMY, WHY ARE PEOPLE
DIFFERENT COLORS?**
by Barbara Knoll.
ISBN 1-56043-156-3

**MOMMY, WAS SANTA CLAUS BORN ON
CHRISTMAS TOO?**
by Barbara Knoll.
ISBN 1-56043-158-X

**MOMMY, WHY DON'T WE
CELEBRATE HALLOWEEN?**
by Linda Hacon Winwood.
ISBN 1-56043-823-1

Available at your local Christian bookstore.

For more information and sample chapters, visit www.destinyimage.com

Adventures in the Kingdom™
Dian Layton

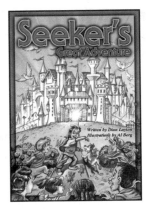

SEEKER'S GREAT ADVENTURE
Seeker and his friends leave the CARNALville of Selfishness and begin the great adventure of really knowing the King!
0-9677402-1-5 • $4.99p

RESCUED FROM THE DRAGON
The King needs an army to conquer a very disgusting dragon and rescue the people who live in the Village of Greed.
0-9677402-2-3 • $4.99p

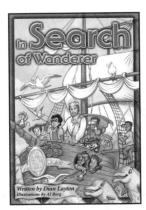

SECRET OF THE BLUE POUCH
The children of the Kingdom explore the pages of an ancient golden book and step through a most remarkable doorway—into a brand new kind of adventure!
0-9677402-7-4 • $4.99p

IN SEARCH OF WANDERER
Come aboard the sailing ship The Adventurer, and find out how Seeker learns to fight dragons through the window of the Secret Place.
0-9677402-8-2 • $4.99p

THE DREAMER
Moira, Seeker's older sister, leaves the Kingdom and disappears into the Valley of Lost Dreams. Can Seeker rescue his sister before it's too late?
0-9707919-4-1 • $4.99p

Available at your local Christian bookstore.

For more information and sample chapters, visit www.destinyimage.com